Why Do We Say THANK YOU?

LEARNING TO BE GRATEFUL

Champ Thornton

Illustrated by Brad Woodard

On a fine, frosty day, in the small town of Kent,
There awoke a young boy who was never content.

"This is boring," he'd say. As if nothing was good.
In his heart, he would never thank God as he should.

If you weighed out his attitude, pail after pail—
You'd have tons of ingratitude . . . (& need a new scale!).

When he talked, he was cross from the first light of day.
Words like "Thanks!" and "That's great!" you would not hear him say.

"The sun's up and shining.
A great day!" went the shout.

"It's too bright; I don't see what the fuss is about."

"Can't you see? It's so good!
Look, just open your eyes.
This day, like all days,
you'll find packed with surprise."

Then Dad cooked a late breakfast. And oh, what a spread!
Stacks of bacon and pancakes as high as your head!

"Let's be thankful," said Dad. Then he prayed for their brunch.
Although what the boy craved was some Choco-Bomb Crunch.

"Aren't you hungry?" Mom asked. "You're not touching your food."

**"Looks too meat-y, too bread-y,
and already chewed."**

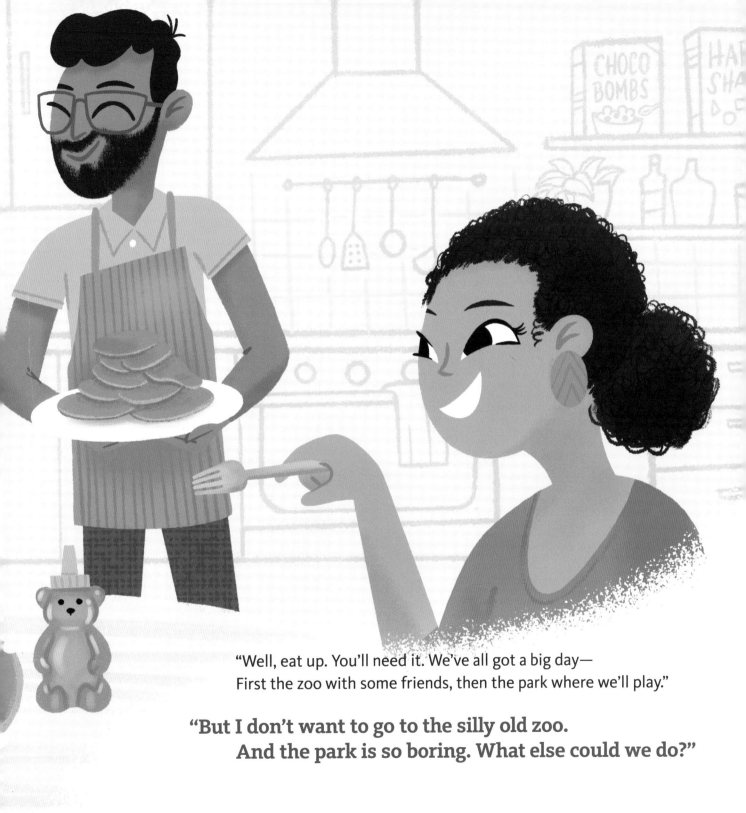

"Well, eat up. You'll need it. We've all got a big day—
First the zoo with some friends, then the park where we'll play."

**"But I don't want to go to the silly old zoo.
And the park is so boring. What else could we do?"**

At the zoo they saw lions,
who stretched while they yawned,

Then three lazy brown bears
swatting flies by a pond.

After this were the snakes.
But he wasn't impressed.
They were curled up in cages,
just getting some rest.

Then he saw a red
woodpecker pecking on wood.
So he pointed and shouted
as loud as he could:

**"Oh wow—look! It's some
bird making holes in a tree.
This whole zoo is as boring as boring can be."**

The boy whined at the birds,
then he sighed at a shark.
And he fussed and he groaned
all the way to Kent Park.

"I just want to go home. There is nothing to see.
This whole drive is as boring as boring can be."

At the park the kids yelled as they ran out to play.
But the boy took his time. He had nothing to say.

The three boys were like brothers, competing to win.
And the girls were both tall, climbing trees in the wind.

"All these kids are so weird,"
thought the boy feeling grumpy.
"Too silly, too speedy, too loud,
and too frumpy."

He just watched as they jumped
between black and white rocks.
Then he plopped down and picked
fuzzy lint from his socks.

"I don't see what's so fun,"
he said, drumming his knee.
"This whole park is as boring as boring can be."

They had fun, minus one, 'til the sun headed down.
Then they got in their cars, zipping home across town.

The boy moped through his meal and while watching TV,

"This whole day's been as boring
                    as boring can be."

"Well, good night. Let's thank God who created all things:
Lord, we're thankful each day, for whatever it brings.

We have blessings from you—we enjoy what you've made.
We can see your own goodness through all things displayed."

After saying Amen, he was ready for bed.
But that prayer kept rolling around in his head.

The boy tossed and he turned—in and out of a dream

And whatever he saw there, was not as it seemed.

It replayed all his day,
but not quite like before.
It was sort of—and like it—
but with something more—

Now wherever he looked,
he was met with surprise.
The true Source of all things
he could see with his eyes!

Whether bacon or plates, God had made all of these—
Giving wheat for the pancakes and syrup from trees!

"Oh wow! Look! God invented the pancakes and bacon! I can see they're from him, if my eyes aren't mistaken."

Now the cobras and pythons
weren't wasting their days,
But God made them cold-blooded
to need the sun's rays.

Now the roar of a lion,
or swipe of a paw
Put a gulp in his throat and
his heart filled with awe.

And the woodpeckers,
well, the boy never had heard
How it captured its food—
the most marvelous bird!

The stiff feathers that make up its tail—are a brace.
When it pecks, the bird's feathers help hold it in place.

And God gave to each one
a thin four-inch-long tongue,
To reach deep-buried bugs
it can feed to its young.

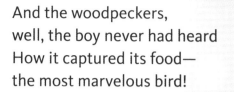

"Oh wow! Look!" thought the boy, "All creation amazes.
Every one of these beasts is a cause to sing praises."

Then he saw, in his dream, all the kids at the park.
But now all was so clear; like bright light in the dark.

All the games came from God! He knew how to have fun.
And the Lord loved each kid; not just those who had won.

In his image the Lord made each girl and each boy.
He had made them unique, and each brought him great joy.

He made fast ones and slow.
He made short ones and tall.
Whether lighter or darker,
he treasures them all.

"Oh wow! Look!" said the boy, "The Lord's helped me to see
That no person is boring—and that includes me!"

The next day there awoke in the small town of Kent,
A young boy who had learned what real thankfulness meant.

He had learned that the Lord made all things very good.
In his heart, he began to thank God as he should.

"The sun's up and shining.
A great day!" went the shout.
(But this time, he had seen
what the fuss was about.)

"I was wrong," said the boy. **"I've been grumpy and bad.
But Christ died to forgive me, and that makes me glad."**

"You're forgiven, our son.
And today's a new start.
We should ask God to help us
give thanks from the heart."

Father, thank you for sky, pecking birds, and all trees.
We are thankful for sunshine and honey from bees.

We say thank you for family and warm loving hugs.
We give thanks for our homes, and hot-chocolate-filled mugs.

And we thank you for church, where we learn and we sing
About Jesus, your Son, and the joy that he brings.

You made everything good; now please open our eyes.
So today, and all days, we'll find packed with surprise.

When you finish this book—stop—give thanks to the Lord.
With the world he has made, there's no cause to be bored.

The whole world's like a window, through which you can see
A Creator who's glorious as glorious can be.

Praise the LORD!
I will give thanks
to the LORD with
my whole heart . . . .
Great are the works
of the LORD, studied
by all who delight
in them.

PSALM 111:1–2

Helping Your Child Learn to Be Thankful

Boredom, complaining, and ingratitude often go hand in hand. Helping your child overcome these bad attitudes involves two things—seeing the wonder and goodness of what God has created and trusting the forgiveness we have in Jesus.

When a child feels **bored**, they're often being passive or just plain lazy. They want to enjoy having something fun, new, or entertaining served to them without work or inconvenience. But if they stop and take a good look around, they will easily notice some of the wonderful things God has made (Psalm 8:1–4; 111:2).

When a child **complains**, you're probably not surprised. If we're honest, we can all admit that when we're bored, even as adults, it's easy to complain. In contrast, when we are truly enjoying what God has made, his good gifts are intended to fill our hearts with delight (Acts 14:17; 1 Timothy 6:17).

And when a child is **ungrateful**, as when they are bored, they're not recognizing that every created thing comes from God (1 Chronicles 29:14). Thankfulness, by comparison, acknowledges the Source of every good thing, enjoys the gift, and thanks the Giver (Psalm 147:7–8; Mark 8:6–8).

The attitudes of **boredom, complaining,** and **ingratitude** are often interconnected. Sometimes not being thankful is expressed through feeling bored and then complaining. These attitudes may reflect that someone is having a bad day. But at heart, they may also signal that one is missing the connection between **the Creator and his creation.** Unbelievers shut their eyes to the Source of the world they live in (Romans 1:21). But God intends his people to enjoy what he's made, to recognize why they enjoy it (because he made it), and to give him thanks.

But what if we *are* having a bad day? Often, it's the hard times that expose what's really in our hearts—and, like the grumpy boy in the story, it's not pretty (Psalm 66:10; 1 Peter 1:6–7). Not being thankful comes from turning away from the Lord and going our own way—what the Bible calls sin (Isaiah 53:6; Romans 1:21). The result? We get grumpier and grumpier. And we complain more and more.

Yet hard times are meant to send us to Jesus for help when we are in trouble and for forgiveness when we respond to trouble by going our own way (Psalm 34:17; 1 John 1:8–9). Jesus came to save us from all the ways we go our own way—including grumbling and complaining. So even in hard times we can always be thankful that Jesus is near and that he forgives our sins. Learning to be thankful at all times opens our eyes to the goodness that is all around us (1 Thessalonians 5:18).

Why Do We Say Thank You? uses a fun and fantastical dream to help your child visualize the connection between the goodness of the Creator and the goodness of his creation. In day-to-day life, outside this book, we don't actually see beams of light illustrating this connection. But your child can use their senses to experience God's creation, and see the connection between God and his world *through faith* (2 Corinthians 5:7).

Here are six ways to help your child learn to say thank you:

1 **Take a "praise pause."** With your child, stop at various times in the day and give ten seconds of thanks and praise to God for something you've seen and enjoyed or admired.

2 **Ask "Who made that?"** When you see your child doing something enjoyable (playing, eating, singing, laughing), ask them who made the thing or activity they're enjoying? ("Who made your leg muscles for running?" "Who made the ice cream so good?")

3 **Create thank-you notes.** Work with your child to make crafts or art projects that compliment neighbors, friends, or family—and thank God for specific things about them.

4 **Use a thank-you string.** Take a length of light-colored yarn or string for your child to hold up and connect to various objects that God made. Then, like the streams of light in this book, children can "see" that God made everything and give thanks.

5 **Teach "beside" prayers.** For example, we often give thanks for our food, but what about the items all around the meal? Help your children say thank you for forks, plates, tables, water, etc.

6 **Teach your children to be thankful they are forgiven.** It's so important to remind your children that we will all fail in being thankful, but because of Jesus's sacrifice for us, we can be forgiven as soon as we ask. Even on a bad day (or maybe *especially* on a bad day!), all who love Jesus can be thankful for forgiveness and eternal life.

God made everything in life to display his own goodness and beauty. So everything is created to delight us. That is **Why**, when we see and enjoy what God has made, **We Say Thank You.**

New Growth Press, Greensboro, NC 27401

Text Copyright © 2022 by George Thomas Thornton II

Illustration Copyright © 2022 by Brad Woodard

Cover/Interior Design: Brad Woodard

ISBN: 978-1-64507-214-0

Library of Congress Cataloging-in-Publication Data on file

Printed in India

29 28 27 26 25 24 23 22   1 2 3 4 5